The Best Pet

Written by Penny Matthews
Illustrated by Beth Norling

An easy-to-read SOLO
for beginning readers

Scholastic Canada Ltd.
New York Toronto London Auckland Sydney
Mexico City New Delhi Hong Kong

Scholastic Canada Ltd.
175 Hillmount Road, Markham, Ontario, Canada L6C 1Z7
Scholastic Inc.
555 Broadway, New York, NY 10012, USA
Scholastic Australia Pty Limited
PO Box 579, Gosford, NSW 2250, Australia
Scholastic New Zealand Limited
Private Bag 94407, Greenmount, Auckland, New Zealand
Scholastic Ltd.
Villiers House, Clarendon Avenue, Leamington Spa,
Warwickshire CV32 5PR, UK

Text copyright © Penny Matthews 1997.
Illustrations copyright © Beth Norling 1997.

Cover design by Lyn Mitchell.
All rights reserved.

First published by Omnibus Books, part of the
SCHOLASTIC GROUP, Sydney, Australia.

National Library of Canada Cataloguing in Publication Data
Matthews, Penny, 1945-
    The best pet
(Solo reading)
ISBN 0-439-98881-0
I. Norling, Beth   II. Title.   III. Series.
PZ7.M373Be 2001   j823   2001-900544-X

5 4 3 2 1   Printed and bound in Canada   1 2 3 4 / 0

For Philip and all his animals – P.M.

*For Custard, Peggy and Jack,
the four-leggeds in our life – B.N.*

Chapter 1

Tom had lots of pets. He had two white mice, Bib and Bub. He had Archie, the praying mantis. He had three tanks of fish. And he had an old tabby cat, Cleo.

Tom loved looking after all his pets. But he couldn't play with them – not really.

Bib and Bub hid in their mouse nest all day long.

Archie hung upside-down in his jar and ate flies.

The fish swam up and down.

And all Cleo did was sleep.

Tom wanted a pet he could play with.

Chapter 2

"My Uncle Fred has ferrets," said Amy at school one day.

"Ferrets?" said Tom. "What's a ferret?"

"Ferrets are smart," said Amy.
"They have soft fur, and they can
run fast. Uncle Fred has a little
one to give away, free."

"Can you have them for pets?"
asked Tom.

"They make the best pets,"
said Amy. "They like playing
hide-and-seek."

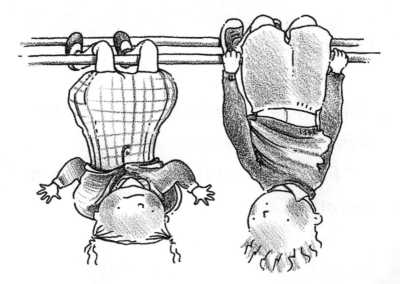

Chapter 3

"I want a ferret," said Tom at breakfast next day. "Ferrets are fun, and they make good pets."

Mum made a face. "Ferrets bite," she said. "What if it bit the baby? And they smell."

"And they run up the leg of your pants when you aren't looking," said Dad.

"Amy's uncle has one to give away, free," said Tom.

"How could we keep a ferret here?" said Mum. "We live in an apartment, not on a farm."

"They don't need much room," said Tom. "Please can I have one?"

"I don't know," said Mum. "I'd like to see it first. Now eat your toast and get ready for school."

Chapter 4

On Saturday Tom went round to Amy's house. Her Uncle Fred was there.

"So you want a ferret," he said to Tom.

Uncle Fred had a box. He lifted the lid. "This is Monty," he said.

Tom saw a small face. A face with bright eyes and round furry ears.

Monty put his front paws on the
edge of the box. They were big
paws, with strong, sharp claws.
He squeaked at Tom.

Tom smiled. "He wants to play with me!" he said.

"Did you ask your mum and
dad if you could keep him?"
asked Uncle Fred.

"Yes," said Tom. "But Mum said
she'd like to see him first. So can
I please take him home now?"

"OK," said Uncle Fred. "If
he gets hungry, give him some
cat food."

Chapter 5

Tom carried the box into his
bedroom. Cleo was on the chair.

"Look Cleo," Tom said. "I've
got a new pet."

Tom opened the box, and
Monty jumped out on to the bed.
   Cleo took one look and ran out
of the room, fast.

Monty stood up on his back legs
and squeaked at Tom.

"You're hungry," said Tom. "I'll
get you some food." He put
Monty back in the box.

First Tom went into the living
room. Mum was feeding the baby,
and Dad was asleep on the sofa.

"Mum," said Tom. "I've got something to show you."
"Not now, Tom," said Mum.

"But it's something you want to see," said Tom.
"Show me later," said Mum.

Tom went to the fridge and put some cat food on a plate.

He took the plate back to his bedroom.

"Dinner, Monty," he said.

Oh, no! The box was empty.

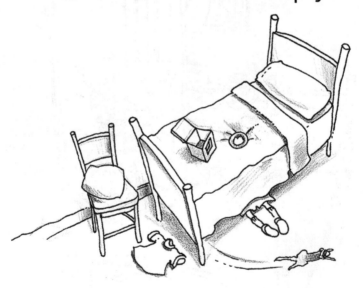

Tom looked under the bed.

He looked in the pile of clothes
on the floor.

He even looked to see if Monty
had climbed up the curtains.

He did find something Monty
had left behind.
But Monty himself had gone.

Chapter 6

Tom raced into the kitchen. No Monty.

Cleo was there, with her tail all fluffed up. *Meow*, she said to Tom.

"Not now, Cleo," said Tom.

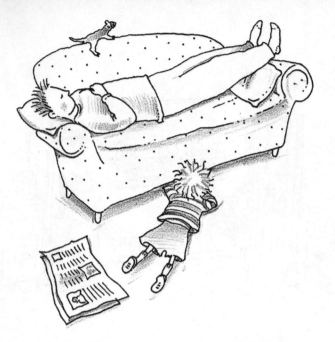

In the living room, he looked under the sofa.

Behind the TV.

On top of the bookcase.

Under the rug.
"Monty," he called softly.

There was a loud crash. The
bathroom!

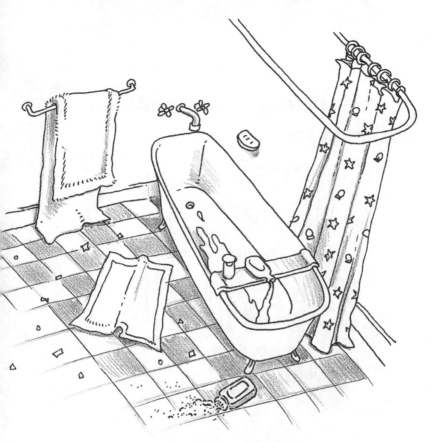

What a mess! Baby powder
was spilled everywhere. Soap
had sharp teeth marks in it.
Shampoo dripped into the bath.
Torn toilet paper was all over
the floor like snow.

White powdery footprints led
out the door.

Chapter 7

There were more footprints in
the laundry.

Potted plants were tipped over
in the hall.

Milk was spilled on the kitchen
floor.

Cleo was acting crazy. *Meow,* she said. *Meow.*

Mum came into the kitchen, and saw the milk on the floor. "Cleo!" she said. "Bad cat!"

She picked Cleo up and put her out the back door.

"Monty!" hissed Tom. "Stop playing hide-and-seek! I give up! Where are you?"

Chapter 8

"Help!" shouted Dad.

Mum came running. Tom came running.

"It's a rat!" shouted Dad.

Thud! Thump!

"Get it out!" Dad yelled. "It's running up my pants!"

"Don't be afraid, Dad," Tom said. "It's only Monty."

Out of Dad's sweater popped a
small face. A face with bright eyes
and round furry ears.

Dad looked at Monty.
Monty looked at Dad.

"*Who* did you say it was?" asked Dad.

"It's Monty, Dad," said Tom. "He's a ferret." He picked Monty up. "Mum said she wanted to see him, and here he is."

"He has a very sweet little face," said Mum.

"Hmm," said Dad, rubbing his leg. "He has very sharp little claws."

Mum sniffed Monty's head. "He doesn't smell," she said.

"He *does* run up the leg of your pants when you aren't looking," said Dad.

"He doesn't bite," said Tom.
"And he doesn't take up much
room. Please can I keep him?"

Chapter 9

"He'll need a lot of looking after," said Dad.

"I look after *all* my pets," said Tom.

Monty squeaked. He stood on his back legs and looked at Mum and Dad.

"I think he likes us," said Mum, smiling at Dad. "OK, Tom. You can keep him."

"Hooray!" said Tom. "Thanks, Mum. Thanks, Dad."

He took Monty back to his bedroom, and showed him to Bib and Bub, and Archie, and the fish.

"Look," he said. "Monty is coming to stay."

Bib and Bub hid in their mouse nest.

Archie ate a fly.

The fish swam up and down.

Tom gave Monty a hug. Monty
squeaked again. He jumped out
of Tom's arms and dashed for the
door. Tom made a grab for him,
but he was too late.

"Oh, *Monty*!" said Tom.

Penny Matthews

My son has had lots of pets – fish, finches,
hermit crabs, and of course our lovely old
cat. He once had a baby praying mantis
and fed it with flies every day. It grew
very big! He has always wanted a ferret,
but never had one, so I wrote this story
for him and gave it a happy ending.

Tame ferrets are clever, and great fun –
but they do need a lot of looking after, so
a ferret may not be *your* best pet!

Beth Norling

Here are some of the many pets my family and I have had over the years. I haven't put in all the goldfish or any of the silkworms because they are too small!

I had to look at many pictures of ferrets before I drew Monty, the pet in this story, to get him looking just right.

I have just had my first baby, and he doesn't sleep a lot, so I've drawn Tom's mum and dad looking a bit tired with *their* new baby. I know how they feel!